MICHAEL DAHL'S
REALLY SCARY STORIES

Raintree is an imprint of Capstone Global Library Limited, a company
incorporated in England and Wales having its registered office at 7 Pilgrim
Street, London, EC4V 6LB – Registered company number: 6695582

www.raintree.co.uk
myorders@raintree.co.uk

Text © Capstone Global Library Limited 2016
The moral rights of the proprietor have been asserted.

Designed by Hilary Wacholz
Original illustrations © Capstone Global Library 2016
Image Credits: Dmitry Natashin
Printed in China

ISBN 978-1-4747-0751-0 (paperback)
19 18 17 16 15
10 9 8 7 6 5 4 3 2 1

ISBN 978-1-4747-0756-5 (ebook pdf)

British Library Cataloguing in Publication Data
A full catalogue record for this book is available from the British Library.

THE STRANGE
VOICE
AND OTHER SCARY TALES

By Michael Dahl

Illustrated by
Xavier Bonet

raintree
a Capstone company — publishers for children

CONTENTS

Dear Reader,

My friend Thom invited me to an unusual Halloween party.

Each guest had to bring a scary story to read. There were only seven of us. After dinner, Thom lit candles and then turned out the lights.

One by one, the guests told their tales.

Some stories were from comics, some from books. One guest had printed his out from the computer. My story was the true tale of a haunted coal mine. Each story gave us goose bumps.

You, too, have been invited to a party. By opening this book you have accepted the invitation. Don't worry if you didn't bring your own scary story. There are plenty here.

You don't need to turn out the lights, either.

THE GOOSE BUMPS WILL STILL COME.

Michael Dahl

DON'T MAKE A WISH

Nina stood up and faced her giant chocolate birthday cake.

"Make a wish! Make a wish!" her friends shouted. They crowded around the table to get a good look at the birthday girl.

Nina's mum and dad stood near by, smiling, presents in their arms.

"Make a wish, sweetie," said her mum.

Nina thought hard. Wishes were serious. She bent towards the nine candles and blew.

"Yeah!" everyone shouted. The candles went out.

But a breeze kept blowing. A strong breeze. It blew across the table, fluttering napkins and shoving aside balloons. Party hats went flying. Birthday presents tumbled onto the floor. The wind whistled louder and louder.

Nina didn't move. She stood still, confetti and streamers swirling around her. "It's coming true," she said.

Nina's mum fought against the wind to reach her side. "What are you talking about?" she yelled. "What did you wish for?"

"I wished Great-Aunt Sally could come to my birthday party," Nina said.

"No, darling," said her mum. "Your Great-Aunt Sally died last week. Don't you remember?"

The doorbell rang.

"Someone's at the door!" yelled a child.

Nina's parents frowned. Was it a late party guest?

Dad marched towards the door.

The wind grew stronger. It rushed against the huge birthday cake.

"No one's out here," Nina's dad called out.

Icing slid down the sides of the cake. The candles flew into the air. The top of the cake exploded, pushed up from inside. Up rose a round white skull, dripping with chocolate. It turned to face Nina.

"Happy birthday, dear," said the skull. "I didn't think I'd make it."

HAIKUKU

The minute arrives.

Door opens – I run! I scream!

The clock pulls me back.

BLINK!

The eye doctor puts drops in my eyes.

"This won't hurt," he says. And he's right. It doesn't hurt at all. There's a funny stinging on my eyeballs, but that's all.

"This is a new medicine," he says. "It should clear up that infection really quickly."

He's talking about the strange eye infection I got at school. Lots of children were getting it and even a few teachers. It makes green goo come out of your eyes, and everything looks fuzzy. So my mum took me to see our eye doctor, Dr Glass, this morning. I know. Glass. Funny, right?

"Don't rub your eyes for at least an hour," says the doctor.

My mum is leading me out of the office when Dr G. stops us. "Oh, one other thing, Kevin," he says to me. "There's a little side effect."

"Side effect?" I repeat.

"You might feel a little dizzy," Dr Glass says as he carefully reads the label on the bottle of medicine he dropped into my eyes just a minute ago.

Didn't he read it before? I wonder. And suddenly I'm not feeling great about my visit.

"It seems you'll have double vision," he says. "It should wear off in a few hours. Nothing to worry about."

"Double vision?" I ask. I'm about to say, *What does that mean?* But suddenly I'm staring at two doctors, each holding a bottle in their right hand. *Okay,* I think. *I know what it means.*

My mum leads me out of the doctor's office, down the corridor and into the lift. I hate lifts, but Dr Glass's office is on the twenty-third floor of the medical building in town. There's no way

I'd be able to climb down twenty-three flights of stairs.

My eyes feel hot. I start to rub them, but then my mum says, "Remember what the doctor said. Don't rub your eyes."

"They itch," I reply.

"Try not to think about it," she says.

"I'm *not* thinking about it," I say. "And they still itch."

"Hush!" she says, glancing around the lift. She's looking at the two other passengers, embarrassed.

I close my eyes, but they start to sting. When I open them again, the lift has two more passengers.

Very odd. I don't remember the lift stopping. I didn't hear the little ding it makes when it stops at a floor. I didn't hear the footsteps of people getting on.

My eyes are hot, so I blink again. Now I see eight people in the lift. *Oh yeah, double vision,* I remind myself. *My eyes are playing tricks.*

But the people in the lift are acting oddly. I hear a woman gasp. A man says, "Let me off! Now!"

Blink.

Now the lift is almost full. And what's even stranger, there are lots of people wearing the same clothes. Almost like they're clones or something.

At first I thought it was just my eyes acting strangely because of the drops. But people are starting to cram in tighter and tighter, so maybe there really are more people in the lift.

Blink.

Without warning, I'm shoved up against the wall.

"Where are all these people coming from?" cries my mother.

And I realize I'm not only *seeing* doubles. There *are* doubles. Doubles of doubles. The number of passengers is doubling, and then doubling again. Each time I blink, more people pop into view. It isn't my eyes. It's really happening.

This is the most amazing thing that has ever happened to me. I can't help myself. I have to look again.

Blink.

Not a good idea.

I get pushed into a corner of the lift. The air is stuffy, and someone just farted. Great.

"Push the stop button!" someone yells.

"Move your elbow!" says another.

"I can't reach the buttons," says a third. "It's too crowded."

How many people are there? How many bodies can the lift hold? At least it feels like the lift is still going down.

Thud.

The lift stops. We're stuck between floors!

"Kevin!" I hear my mum's voice.

"I'm back here," I reply. I don't dare to look at her. I keep my eyes squeezed shut.

Four men near the front of the lift all say at

the same time, "We're on the main floor. This is the lobby. But the doors won't open."

Four women say, "Push the Open button."

Four more women say, "Can whoever is farting please stop?"

Eight men say, "It wasn't me!"

It's getting harder to breathe. We're running out of air. I can feel bodies squirming around. I can hear people crying, shouting, moaning, giggling. (Some people are ticklish, I suppose.)

"Kevin!" My mum's voice is getting weaker.

"I'm going to faint," a man next to me says.

Somewhere a woman whispers, "What we need is more force to open those doors."

Force! I think. More and more power pushing against the doors. This gives me an idea. It might be foolish, but I decide we can't stay in the lift much longer. We need to get out one way or another.

I open my eyes.

I look at as many people as I can. Then I blink. And I keep on blinking.

More and more bodies fill the lift. Bodies on top of bodies. Screaming bodies. Squirming bodies. The ceiling light is covered up, then it gets smashed in the squeeze. My knees are giving out from all the extra people weighing me down. The air is being sucked up faster and faster by the extra pairs of lungs.

A long, drawn-out groan shakes the lift. And then – *bang!* – the crush of people burst the lift doors apart. It worked! We spill out into the lobby like sweets from a gumball machine.

My mum finds me after a few minutes. She hugs me and then grabs my arm and walks me outside.

"My eyes hurt!" I say. "I can't open them."

"That's fine, sweetie," she says.

She gets us onto a bus and back home safely, guiding me the whole way.

Alone in my room, I feel my way over to the bed. I decide I'll lie down, pull the covers over my head and rest. Dr Glass said the double vision would last a few hours. If I go to sleep now, when I wake up in the morning everything should be back to normal.

My feet hit something as I walk across the floor, and I stumble. My eyes fly open. Oh no!

I was looking at my bed when I fell. It didn't double. It looks a little fuzzy around the edges, but otherwise it has stayed the same.

That was lucky, I think. I sit on the edge of the bed and stare across the room at my dresser. The dresser with the mirror.

Blink.

Big mistake.

Too bad there aren't two beds in my room. I could use them now.

I mean, *we* could.

SNOW MONSTER

The Sun was low in the sky. The clouds were so orange, they looked like they were on fire. There was a light breeze. The snow had stopped falling. It was perfect hunting weather.

Deer come out just before the Sun sets. And there are a lot of deer where we live, just outside a small town in northern Wisconsin, USA. North of our home there's a line of evergreens, which is the border of a large forest. Lots of deer trails lead into the trees. We were following one that morning.

I love being out in the woods with my father. When I was really young, he taught me how to recognize an animal's footprints.

In the woods that morning I could see the tracks of rabbits, fox, field mice and, of course, deer.

It was cold enough to see our breath, but not too cold. Carefully and quietly we headed deep into the woods. We came to a small clearing. My father stopped suddenly.

He was looking down at the snow. "We'd better go back, son," he said.

"What is it?" I asked.

He shook his head and turned away, but I had to see. I ran over and looked at the snow. There were footprints I had never seen before. They were huge – at least four times bigger than my father's.

I looked at him. *The Geeshee Moogomon?* I wondered.

I had heard the stories. The Geeshee was a big, bloodthirsty beast that could change its shape and colour. You never saw it until it was too late. It was a story adults told us to keep us from going into the deep woods. To keep us out of trouble. I'd never believed it was real.

My father was firm. "We're going home," he said. "Now."

Suddenly, I saw what else my father had seen. The dead body. A deer had fallen onto the snow. Blood spread out from it, red staining the white ground.

A scream pierced the air. A nearby tree seemed to explode. Bark flew off and hit my head.

"Hurry!" cried my father.

We both turned and took off across the snow, our tails flying behind us. I never looked back.

After several minutes, my father stopped. He lifted his head and howled. We had to warn our cousins and neighbours of the danger.

We took the long way home. "So the Geeshee won't be able to find us," my father said.

When we were finally inside our den, I raced to my mother. I snuggled as close as I could, hearing her heart beat beneath her beautiful fur.

For now, I was safe from the monster.

A PERFECT FIT

Fitting in. That's the hardest part about going to a new school, Lola thought.

New classrooms, new teachers, new locker – all of it was hard at first. But fitting in and finding new friends was the worst.

And the worst part of fitting in, Lola thought, *is working out where to sit for lunch.* It was the biggest decision of her first day. Lola couldn't afford to make a mistake.

Standing near the wall of the canteen, Lola held her lunch tray and looked around. She was too new to have made any friends. No one expected her to sit with them. Lola was afraid to sit just anywhere. What if she sat at the wrong table? With the wrong children, children who also didn't fit in? For the rest of her school life, she would be known as a loser.

"Hey! Hey you!" Lola saw a girl in a bright-yellow jumper waving at her. She slowly walked over to the girl's table.

"You mean *me*?" asked Lola.

"Sit down," said the girl in the yellow jumper. "I'm Jordan." Then she introduced the other four girls at the table: Eva, Anna, Lillian and Kate.

"And what is your name?" asked Jordan.

"Lola," she said, shyly.

"Lola? That's different," said Anna.

The girl named Lillian giggled.

"It's Spanish," said Eva. "Or Mexican."

"Oh. Are you, like, Spanish?" asked Kate.

Eva rolled her eyes.

"No," said Lola. "My mum just liked the name."

Jordan nodded. "It's very Hollywood," she said.

Lunchtime passed quickly. The girls talked about classes and teachers and what they had done over the summer holidays. The canteen bell rang. Lola looked up at the caged clock. Lunch break was over? She was having so much fun that she hadn't noticed the time.

"Time to go, girls," said a teacher as she walked by.

When they got up from the table, Lola noticed something for the first time. Something odd. Each girl had the same rucksack. The rucksacks were purple with white trim. Some of the girls had decorated theirs with stickers and key rings and buttons, but it was the same rucksack.

As she gathered her own bag, Lola realized that all the girls had worn them while they ate. None of them had taken their rucksacks off.

Maybe they're a club, thought Lola. *And that's, like, their uniform or something.*

"See ya," said Lola, with a little wave.

"Bye!" they all replied brightly. The five girls

turned and walked away from the table. Five purple rucksacks disappeared into the crowd of pupils.

For the next week, Lola always sat at the same table. She sometimes saw her lunch friends in the halls. She had lessons with a few of them. Jordan (the girl who had waved at her), Anna, Eva, Lillian and Kate. No matter where she saw them, they always wore their rucksacks. Even while sitting in class.

What about PE class? Lola wondered. *They would have to put them in their lockers then, right?*

One day, Lola heard two other girls in the hall talking about her friends.

"Those rucksack girls are so fake," said one.

"They act all sweet," agreed the other one. "But then they say things behind your back."

Lola didn't think her new friends were fake. They had gone out of their way to be nice to her, to make her feel welcome. And they didn't gossip any more than everyone else did. Those girls in the hall were just jealous.

During Friday's lunch, when all the girls were seated, Anna leaned into the table and whispered, "Tomorrow night – sleepover!"

"Cool!"

"Yeah!"

"Fun!" the girls whispered back.

Jordan turned to Lola and said, "You're coming, right?"

"Oh, uh–" said Lola.

"Of course she's coming," said Anna.

Lola couldn't believe her luck. The first week of school was over, and she already had a group of cool friends. And now a sleepover party. Lola and her mother went shopping that night and bought a new sleeping bag. Lola insisted on a rucksack, too. She picked out a purple one. It wasn't the same brand the other girls had, but it was the right size. Lola liked the way it felt on her shoulders. She was sure it would help her fit in.

On Saturday night, Lola's dad drove her to Anna's house. "Have fun, sweetie!" he yelled to her as she ran towards the front door.

The other girls were already there. The party was filled with loud music, laughter, pizza, ice cream and gossip. The entire night, even as the girls laid out their sleeping bags in the big family room at the back of the house, Jordan and her friends never took off their rucksacks. Lola tried keeping hers on, but after a while it became uncomfortable.

In fact, Jordan came up to her during a break in the fun and helped Lola slip it off her shoulders. "It's not the same kind," she said to Lola.

Lola felt like someone had hit her in the stomach. *Those two girls in the hall were right,* she thought, her eyes filling with tears.

"What's wrong?" Kate asked, walking over to them.

These girls don't really like me, thought Lola. *I need to go. I'll call Dad to come and pick me up.*

"Her rucksack," Jordan told Kate.

"Is that all?" Kate took Lola's hand. "Don't worry about it," she said. "We can help you find another one. Jordan's the queen of bargain stores, and I'm the queen of key rings!"

Jordan smiled at Lola. "You look good in purple, too," she said.

Lola wiped her eyes and smiled back. "Thanks," she said.

It was nearing midnight and all the girls were dressed for sleep, sitting or lying on their sleeping bags. The purple rucksacks were still on their shoulders. Lola felt better. They were all talking and laughing when Anna's mother yelled down the hallway, "Lights out, girls!"

Anna rolled her eyes. "You heard her," she whispered. "Lights out, girls." The rest of them giggled.

With the lights off, the family room was surprisingly dark. As Lola snuggled into her sleeping bag, she heard rustling all around her. The girls were taking off their rucksacks. *Finally,* thought Lola. Then it was quiet.

Lola woke up an hour later, needing to use the bathroom. Too much fizzy drink. She slipped out of her sleeping bag as quietly as she could and stood up in the dark. The other girls were sleeping. Someone was snoring. Someone else was mumbling in her sleep.

Lola remembered where the bathroom was and walked down the short corridor. On her way back, she snapped off the bathroom light and then stood still. Her eyes needed a few moments adjusting from the bright bathroom to the dark corridor. She didn't want to trip or fall over anyone.

Where was her sleeping bag? She stepped carefully, as if she were walking on the balance beam in the gym. Her foot hit someone's back.

"Oops. Sorry," she said.

Lola's eyes were growing more used to the dark. She could see the five shapes of the sleeping girls. She saw her empty sleeping bag. She looked down at the girl she had bumped into. It was Jordan.

Lola bent down. "Sorry," she whispered again. But Jordan didn't move.

Something about the position of her arms bothered Lola. She didn't know why, but she reached out to the sleeping girl and gently touched her arm.

It was cold. Not freezing cold, but it certainly wasn't giving off any warmth. It felt like plastic.

Lola heard the mumbling again. It came from beyond the circle of sleeping bags.

She spotted a shadow next to the wall. A pile of dark purple. *The rucksacks,* Lola thought. That's where the girls had put them. But who was mumbling in her sleep?

Lola watched in terror as one of the rucksacks moved. It swayed back and forth. It waddled across the carpet like a penguin. The shoulder straps hung on either side like skinny arms. A thin white line appeared on the front of the rucksack. A fold in the purple fabric. A fold that seemed to turn into a smile.

"Don't worry," whispered the rucksack. "We'll find one for you, Lola." It was Jordan's voice.

Lola was about to scream when she felt something soft and bumpy brush against her leg. She glanced down and saw more rucksacks. The one nearest her leg opened its mouth and Lola could see rows and rows of tiny, sharp teeth.

"We'll help you find a new one. The right one," said the rucksack.

The rucksack's voice was Lola's voice.

Lola fell onto her sleeping bag. The purple creature shuffled towards her and patted her back. "Yes, yes. A new rucksack," it said gently. "She will be a perfect fit."

PAVEMENTS FROM OUTER SPACE

What a film! I mean, what a *film*!

We burst out of the cinema – my friend Carl and I, and my big brother, Sam, and his buddy Ethan. We couldn't stop talking about it.

"So cool!" Carl said.

"Totally amazing," I said.

Stealth Invasion IV: Alien Destruction. Best. Film. Ever. The absolute best in the series.

"I want to see it again," said Sam.

"We are so seeing it again," said Carl.

"I can't," said Ethan. "Gotta get home. It's late."

It was late. After midnight. The Moon and stars were shining. My mum and Carl's parents had let us stay out late because we were with Sam and Ethan, who were sixteen.

We walked down the pavement, past a corner where people were getting on a city bus. Its doors hissed shut as it pulled away from the kerb. The greenish lights inside the bus and the tinted windows made the passengers inside look like aliens. Visitors to our planet were taking off in their silver ship. *Swoosh!*

"The alien destructor suits were cool!" I said.

"Their blue starships were even cooler," said Carl.

Sam snorted. "Which is why the whole thing would never work," he said. "Not in real life. Not in a million years."

"Yeah," said Ethan.

I stopped walking. "What do you mean?" I said.

"Alien invasion," said Sam. "If their ships were coming at us like that, in the open, we would have seen them from miles away."

"The armies of Earth would have banded together," said Ethan. "By the time they reached the planet, we'd be ready for them."

"We sure wouldn't be surprised, like the soldiers in the film," said Sam. "The film is called *Stealth Invasion*. Where was the stealth part?"

"Good one, Sam," agreed Ethan.

We started walking again. We were ten minutes from our house. Carl was sleeping over with us, but Ethan lived a little further away. The four of us were the only ones on the pavement. I could feel warmth rising from the cement, even though the night was cool. Cool and dark. And each street got darker than the last. Why weren't the streetlights working?

Ethan was chuckling to himself. I suppose he was still thinking about Sam's remark that the aliens weren't stealthy. Sam sort of had a point.

"If you're so clever, how would you do it?" asked Carl.

"Yeah, how would you do it?" I said.

Sam usually waves his arms around when

he talks big. This time he didn't. He stopped in the middle of the street, where the shadows were thickest. He leaned in close to us, like he didn't want anyone else to hear. "Like the film says, boys – stealth," Sam said. "Hidden. Secret. Camouflaged."

"I know what stealth means," I said.

"If I were an alien, I'd already be here," said Sam. "I would have been here for years by now. Many years. Hiding. Just waiting for the right time. Then I'd attack and catch everyone by surprise. That's how an invasion works."

"Good one, Sam," said Ethan.

"Where would you hide?" Carl asked quietly.

Sam looked around. He stared down at his shoes. He snorted again. "We don't know what aliens really look like, right?" he said. "So why couldn't they be disguised as something normal you see everyday?"

"Something normal?" said Ethan seriously.

Sam nodded. "Like ... a pavement."

Carl laughed. Ethan didn't smile.

A pavement, I thought. *Why not?*

"One night," said Sam, "when we were all asleep, the aliens came. The aliens were long like giant snakes. Their scales were hard like cement. They took the place of pavements all over town. All across the country. And all those years while we were walking on them, they were listening and watching us. Learning all about us humans. And we might never ever know."

How long would the aliens wait to attack? I wondered.

"Let's go home," said Carl.

But I had to know more. "When would you attack?" I asked.

"Tonight," said Ethan. "No one would be expecting that. Would they?"

Sam looked at him in surprise.

"You guys are creeping me out," said Carl.

I looked at the pavement. I tried feeling it through my shoes. Was it warmer than normal? Pavements stayed warm after it got dark, because they held all that heat from the Sun.

But was that really the reason, or were they actually alive? I stared at the pavement in the dark. I tried to tell if it was moving. If it was breathing.

Sam was biting his upper lip. I knew that look. He was trying hard not to laugh. I ignored him and looked up at the night sky. There were a lot of shooting stars.

"You guys..." said Carl.

The pavement shook, like an earthquake or something really big was happening. Something really big, but really far away, and just now reaching us.

"We're probably just feeling a lorry go by," said Sam.

"There aren't any lorries on the street," Ethan pointed out. There weren't any cars either. It was dark, and we were the only ones around.

"Can this be happening?" I said.

I looked at the street again. Was Sam right? No one would suspect a pavement. You saw them every day. Wait! I glanced at the corner of the street.

The fire hydrant was glowing. Slowly it stretched up into the air, growing like a strange metal tree.

"That's how they did it!" said Sam. "That's their disguise!"

Ethan stood right behind me, chuckling. "Don't be stupid," he said. "Hydrants aren't alive."

The hydrant grew taller and thicker until it was the size of a car.

Suddenly, Ethan's voice changed. "They're things," he said. "Tools."

I turned around and saw a stranger wearing Ethan's clothes. His body was heavy. His arms ended in claws. His face was green and rubbery. His eyes were just slits, like a cat's.

"What do you see every day?" he said, in a thick, rubbery voice. "Your friends," he went on. "Your neighbours. But do you really know who they are? What they are?"

The stranger came closer, and the three of us, Sam, Carl, and I, backed up further and further.

Something metal clanged. Bars fell in front of

us like a prison cell. We were locked inside the hydrant. It had become a sturdy steel cage.

That's when we heard the sirens go off.

And when we knew the aliens were here.

THE STRANGE VOICE

Logan needed a break from after-school band practice. He needed to go to the toilet. But he hated going when other boys were in there. Logan needed his privacy. Which is why, during the break, he ran down the corridor and found a toilet far away from the band room.

Ah, nice. The cool, dim room was peaceful. Peaceful as a graveyard, his grandma would say.

It was soothing to his ears after the noisy music practice. A loud note ... *fortissimo!* – blasted from the trombone was still pinging through his brain.

He could still hear it, standing in the toilets. No, it was something else.

A strange voice. Talking on a mobile, from one of the stalls.

Great. Someone was in there at the same time! Logan would have to wait until that person left before he could finish his business. He coughed. Then he cleared his throat. Hoping the person heard him and got the message: Hurry up and leave!

But no, the voice kept mumbling and mumbling.

The room was dim. There were no windows. One lightbulb in a wire cage hung from the ceiling. Slowly, Logan bent down and twisted his head to peek under the stalls. He moved carefully. He didn't want to lose his balance so that he'd have to touch the cold cement floor with his bare hands. Gross.

Logan counted the bottoms of three white toilets. No feet.

The boy must be sitting, or standing, on the toilet, talking on the phone, Logan thought.

He stood up and shook his head. He knew practically everyone in the school, but he didn't recognize the voice. The voice was deep, but it wasn't a man's voice. It definitely belonged to a child. An older child.

Logan recognized a few words. It wasn't as if he was trying to hear on purpose. He couldn't help it.

... *mumble ... underground ... things ... mumble ... grave ... mumble ...*

Afraid to make a sound, Logan stood completely still.

... *mumble ... water ... mumble ... water ... mumble ... everywhere ...*

He carefully tiptoed out of the toilets and into the corridor. Then he leaned against the wall and let out his breath. Who *was* that? What was he talking about? And would he ever leave the toilets?

Logan started hopping up and down. This was getting serious. A normal person would have finished their business by now and come out.

He crossed his legs and waited ten more minutes. He knew he should head back to the music room, but he had to go. It was building up inside him like a clogged drain. He was probably already late for the second half of practice anyway.

"Are you kidding me?" Logan cried, throwing up his arms. That was it. He was tired of waiting. Boy or no boy, he was going to use the toilets. He walked back in. He cleared his throat and fake-sneezed so the speaker would hear him. Logan stood still. The voice had stopped.

He glanced down the row of stalls. The doors were swinging open. But he thought the middle door had been shut before.

As Logan walked past the stalls, he realized no one was there. The doors hung open and no one was sitting inside.

Had the voice come from a vent somewhere? Could it have been someone out in the corridor, echoing off the dirty wall tiles?

Logan did what he came to do. Then he stood at the sink and washed his hands.

He heard the voice behind him.

... mumble ... underneath ... mumble ... water ... inside ...

It was coming from the middle stall. Logan shuffled over to the half-open door. He could see the toilet, the silver pipes, the pile of paper towels and the stupid graffiti on the walls. Another mumble came from the toilet itself. Logan took a few more steps.

A mobile phone floated in the water.

Okay. Someone had dropped his phone without realizing it, and his friend was still talking on the other end. Strange. It looked like a nice phone. The owner would want it back. *I'll take it to the lost and found,* thought Logan.

Then he thought, *Why me?*

Then he thought, *Okay, it's only water.* Logan stooped down to pick up the lost, mumbling phone.

A hairless hand reached up from inside the toilet and grabbed him.

It started to pull.

ABOUT THE AUTHOR

Michael Dahl, the author of the Library of Doom and Troll Hunters series, is an expert on fear. He is afraid of heights (but he still flies). He is afraid of small, enclosed spaces (but his house is crammed with over 3,000 books). He is afraid of ghosts (but that same house is haunted). He hopes that by writing about fear, he will eventually be able to overcome his own. So far it is not working. But he is afraid to stop. He claims that, if he had to, he would travel to Mount Doom in order to toss in a dangerous piece of jewelry. Even though he is afraid of volcanoes. And jewellery.

ABOUT THE ILLUSTRATOR

Xavier Bonet is an illustrator and comic-book
artist who resides in Barcelona. Experienced in
2D illustration, he has worked as an animator
and a background artist for several different
production companies. He aims to create works
full of colour, texture and sensation, using both
traditional and digital tools. His work in children's
literature is inspired by magic and fantasy as well
as his passion for the art.

MICHAEL DAHL TELLS ALL

Do you know how a pearl is formed? A tiny grain of sand or grit gets trapped inside the slippery gut of an oyster. Juices from the oyster stick to the grain and harden, covering it layer by layer. The bit of sand grows into a beautiful shiny glob – a pearl. That's how stories are formed, too. Some tiny idea or inspiration, like a birthday party or a cuckoo clock or a noise in an empty bathroom, gets stuck in my brain. More ideas come along and get stuck to the first idea, building it up layer by layer, sentence by sentence. And the result? A nice spooky glob called a story. Here's where some of the stories in this book began.

DON'T MAKE A WISH

There's an **old saying:** Be careful what you wish for, because it might come true. How bad could a wish be, especially at a fun event like a birthday party? I like to use this formula for scary stories: start with something happy or cheerful, and then see what could possibly go wrong.

HAIKUKU

Making up **haiku**, a form of Japanese poetry, has been a pastime of mine since I learned what they were at the age of 10. Recently I read a scary haiku by the author Katherine Applegate, creator of Animorphs and *The One and Only Ivan*. She inspired me to make my own spooky mini-tale, in only seventeen syllables.

BLINK!

One of my favourite **Doctor Who** episodes is called "Blink". It's about evil statues that move towards you when you're not looking! I challenged myself to think up a story that would be completely different but would have the same name. Blinking made me think of eyes, and that made me think of eye doctors, and that made me think of eye drops. And drops made me think of lifts. Strange, I know. But that's where stories come from.

SNOW MONSTER

One of my favourite kinds of stories is where you're reading along, minding your own business and then someone drops a **plot twist** and – boom! – everything changes. Then you go back and reread the story to find out how you were tricked. Once you know the trick, you can't wait to re-watch the film or reread the book and see how it all fits together. I used the snowy woods as a backdrop because of hunting stories I've heard from friends in Minnesota, Wisconsin and Iowa in the USA.

A PERFECT FIT

Sleepovers are the perfect time for telling scary stories. What if having a sleepover was the scary story? The story's subject came from my memories of school. I always disliked cliques, those special little groups where all the members look and act and sound alike. Are they robots, or worse...?

PAVEMENTS FROM OUTER SPACE

From the age of 9–11, I had a recurring **nightmare about aliens** landing in my garden. My friends and I tried to hide behind trees and bushes, but we were always caught. That's when I woke up, breathing hard and staring out of the window to make sure I didn't see fleets of ships hanging in the night sky. I think I was freaked out after watching the 1953 sci-fi movie *Invaders from Mars* on TV. (Here's a strange note: the film's writer was inspired by a dream his wife had about aliens invading the planet. Hmm. What do you call it when different people have the same dream? Creepy!)

THE STRANGE VOICE

Quiet, **empty toilets** (for boys or girls) are just plain spooky. This story gives one reason why!

GLOSSARY

alien being from another planet

bloodthirsty taking pleasure in violence

destruction something that has been destroyed

disguised concealing something, usually having to do with your appearance

earthquake sudden, violent shaking of the ground, which may damage buildings

gossip talk about other people's personal business

graffiti art or words people put on walls and other surfaces where they're not supposed to be

infection illness caused by bacteria or a virus

introduced made known to other people

invasion attack made on a country or other place

jealous feeling resentful of someone because they have something you want

mumble speak quietly and unclearly

privacy when a person is not seen or disturbed by anyone else

sirens devices that make a loud, shrill noise

stealth secret, clever way of behaving

suspect think something may be true

DISCUSSION QUESTIONS

1. In "Pavements from Outer Space", a group of boys encounters an alien on their walk home from the cinema. What do you think happens after the story ends? Discuss what the alien invasion might look like.

2. Logan hears a voice in the story "The Strange Voice", and he thinks there is another boy in the toilets at the same time as him. Soon he realizes that there's no one there, but the voice continues. If you were in Logan's position, would you have left the toilets earlier? Talk about why or why not.

3. In "Don't Make A Wish", what do you think the wish was that Nina made?

WRITING PROMPTS

1. In the story "A Perfect Fit", Lola is having trouble fitting in at her new school. Have you ever had trouble fitting in? Write a paragraph about it.

2. In "Snow Monster", a father and son are out hunting when they come across signs that the Geeshee Moogomon has been nearby. Imagine you are the monster, and write the story from your point of view.

3. "Haikuku" follows a form of poetry called the haiku. A haiku has three lines. The first line is five syllables, the second is seven syllables and the third is five syllables. Write a spooky haiku of your own!

MICHAEL DAHL'S
REALLY SCARY STORIES